PROJECT

# NOAH'S ARK

# NOAH'S ARK

## Jane Ray

With words from the Authorised King James
Version of the Bible

ORCHARD BOOKS

*For Clara*

Extracts from the Authorised King James Version of the Bible,
the rights of which are vested in the Crown in perpetuity
within the United Kingdom, are reproduced by permission of
Eyre & Spottiswoode Publishers, Her Majesty's Printers, London.

ORCHARD BOOKS
96 Leonard Street, London EC2A 4RH
*Orchard Books Australia*
14 Mars Road, Lane Cove, NSW 2066
ISBN 1 85213 206 X (hardback)
ISBN 1 85213 947 1 (paperback)
First published in Great Britain 1990
First paperback publication 1995
Illustrations © Jane Ray 1990
A CIP catalogue record for this book
is available from the British Library.
Printed in Belgium

God saw that the wickedness of man was great
in the earth, and it grieved him at his heart.

And God said, I will destroy man, and beast,
and the creeping thing, and the fowls of the air;
for it repenteth me that I have made them.

But Noah was a just man, and Noah walked
with God. And Noah begat three sons, Shem,
Ham and Japheth.

And God said unto Noah, I will cause it to
rain upon the earth forty days and forty nights;
and every thing that is in the earth shall die. But
with thee will I establish my covenant.

Make thee an ark of gopher wood. Rooms
shalt thou make in the ark and shalt pitch it
within and without with pitch. The length of the
ark shall be three hundred cubits, the breadth

fifty cubits, and the height of it thirty cubits.

A window shalt thou make; and the door of the ark shalt thou set in the side thereof; with lower, second, and third stories shalt thou make it.

And thou shalt come into the ark, thou, and thy sons,

and thy wife, and thy sons' wives with thee.

And of every living thing, two of every sort shalt

thou bring into the ark, the male and the female;

of fowls of the air

and of beasts, and of every thing

that creepeth upon the earth.

And take thou unto thee of all food that is eaten; and it shall be for food for thee, and for them. Thus did Noah, according to all that God commanded him.

And it came to pass after seven days that the waters of the flood were upon the earth. The windows of heaven were opened; and the ark went upon the face of the waters.

And all the high hills, that were under the
whole heaven, were covered.

And the mountains were covered.

Every living substance was destroyed which
was upon the ground, both man, and cattle, and
the creeping things, and the fowl of the heaven.

Noah only remained alive, and they that were with him in the ark.

And God remembered Noah, and made a wind to pass over the earth. The rain from heaven was restrained, and the ark rested upon the mountains of Ararat. And the waters decreased continually until the tops of the mountains were seen.

And at the end of forty days Noah opened the
window of the ark and sent forth a dove, to see
if the waters were dried up from off the earth.

But she found no rest for the sole of her foot and
returned into the ark.

And Noah again sent forth the dove; and she came in the evening and in her mouth was an olive leaf: so Noah knew that the waters were abated from off the earth. And at the end of seven days Noah again sent forth the dove, which returned not any more.

And Noah removed the covering of the ark, and
looked, and behold, the face of the ground was dry.
And God spoke unto Noah, saying, I will set
my bow in the cloud, and it shall be a token of a
covenant between me and you and every living creature.

Go forth of the ark, thou and all thy house.
Bring forth with thee every living thing that is
with thee, both of fowl, and of cattle, and of every

creeping thing that creepeth upon the earth.
Be fruitful, and multiply, and replenish the earth.

And while the earth remaineth, seedtime and harvest, and cold and heat, and summer and winter, and day and night shall not cease.